Grandpa I Just Wanna be a Cowboy:

Notables from the West

Books by Trae Q.L. Venerable

Grandpa I Just Wanna be a Cowboy: Notables from the West
Grandpa I Just Wanna be a Cowboy: Rodeo Cowboys
Grandpa I Just Wanna be a Cowboy: Women In the West

Grandpa I Just Wanna be a Cowboy:

Notables from the West

Trae Q.L. Venerable

SPEAKING VOLUMES, LLC
NAPLES, FLORIDA
2017

Grandpa I Just Wanna be a Cowboy:
Notables from the West

ISBN 978-1-62815-710-9

History has defined us for a long time. But now, the truth about the forgotten cowboys will come to the light.

For all of the forgotten cowboys...
- Trae Q. L. Venerable

It was Saturday morning, Bo was happy to go to his grandparent's home for the weekend!

Bo knew what time it was when he arrived at Grandpa LeRoy and Julia Ann's home. He was ready to watch the new western cartoons with his Grandpa LeRoy...

Bo knew today was going to be something special, on this morning....

They were adding a new cowboy to the series and he couldn't wait.

He yelled out at the top of his lungs to his Grandpa,

"I wanna be a cowboy"

"I wanna be a cowboy"

"I just wanna be a cowboy"

While watching his cartoons, Bo's Grandpa brought out an old book to inform Bo on some pretty neat people who helped shape the West.

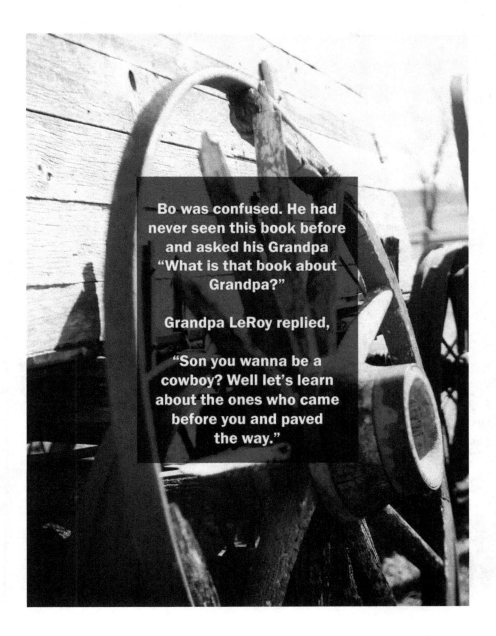

Bo was confused. He had never seen this book before and asked his Grandpa "What is that book about Grandpa?"

Grandpa LeRoy replied,

"Son you wanna be a cowboy? Well let's learn about the ones who came before you and paved the way."

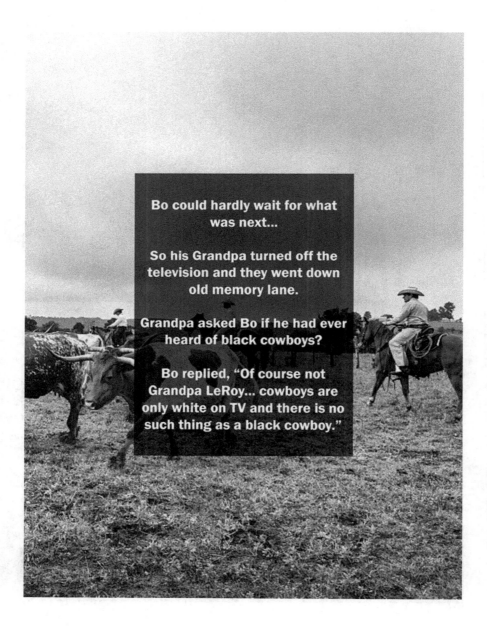

Bo could hardly wait for what was next...

So his Grandpa turned off the television and they went down old memory lane.

Grandpa asked Bo if he had ever heard of black cowboys?

Bo replied, "Of course not Grandpa LeRoy... cowboys are only white on TV and there is no such thing as a black cowboy."

Grandpa replied, "History wants you to think that Bo. However, back in the old days 1 in every 3 cowboys were of African-American descent."

Grandpa said, "Television only shows cowboys like the Lone Ranger but not the other kinds."

Grandpa followed that by saying, "Bo they look just like you!!!"

Bo didn't know how to take this new information. He was so overwhelmed with joy...

Bo begged his Grandpa to tell him more and that is where the fun really begins!

Grandpa calmed Bo down from his excitement and opened the old book to the first notable; Nat Love.

Bo urged his Grandpa LeRoy to tell him more.

Grandpa told Bo, "Nat was an all-around cowboy in the Panhandle of Texas. He was skilled in the cowboy tasks of roping, breaking wild horses, and working cattle drives to major cow towns such as Dodge City, Kansas."

Bo was thrilled about this and begged for more.

Grandpa flipped to a new part and Bill Pickett came up, another notable cowboy.

Bo said, "Why Why Grandpa?"

Grandpa replied, "Bill Pickett was a great cowboy. He was with the 101 Ranch and Wild West Show and also invented the technique rodeo contestants do call 'Bulldogging'."

After Grandpa explained what bulldogging was, Bo started to practice on Smokey the family dog.

After Bo was finished bulldogging Smokey the family dog he was ever so tired.

Grandpa decided to give Bo a few more notable cowboys out of the old book.

He went with John Ware next who was best remembered for his horsemanship and for bringing the first cattle to Southern Alberta, Canada in 1882.

After Grandpa explained this, Bo was truly getting tired but had enough energy to hear about two more cowboys.

Grandpa was thinking and flipped the pages again and Bass Reeves came up.

Grandpa went on, "He was the first black deputy west of the Mississippi River and arrested over 3000 felons. He also shot and killed 14 outlaws in self defense. Bo, he was the real life Lone Ranger. What the Lone Ranger did on TV, Bass Reeves did it in real life."

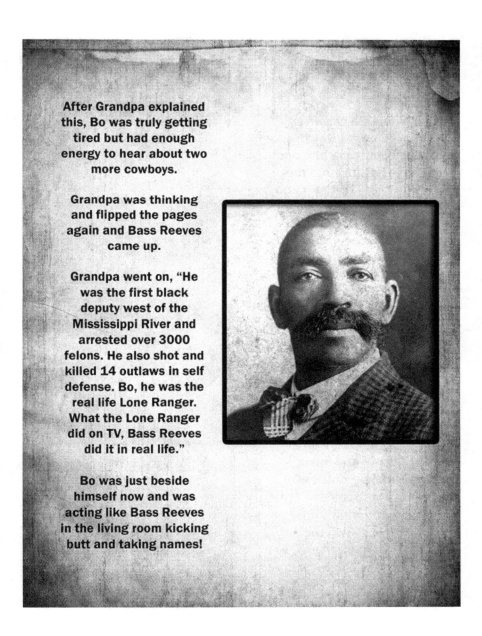

Bo was just beside himself now and was acting like Bass Reeves in the living room kicking butt and taking names!

Since Bo was even more beat after this, Grandpa gave him one last cowboy and this was a guy by the name Isom Dart.

Grandpa told Bo, "Ned Huddleston was his real name. He earned the reputation as a rider, roper, and bronco-buster. Ned earned the nicknames the "Black Fox" and the "Calico Cowboy." Later in his life he joined the infamous Tip Gault Gang. The Tip Gault Gang was a cattle and horse rustling outfit of Southeastern Wyoming."

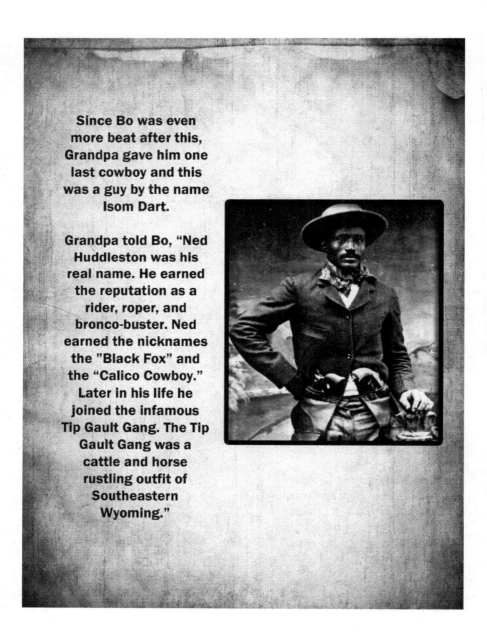

Bo was on the floor now looking up at the ceiling and imagining all of those notable black cowboys and told his Grandpa, "Tell me more after my nap!"

Grandpa agreed. He had the old book in one arm and his new defined black cowboy Bo in the other. He put him to bed and told Bo,

"Until the next time partner."

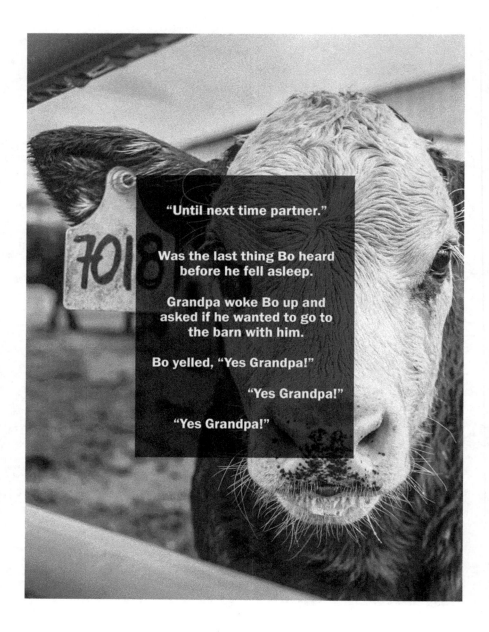

"Until next time partner."

Was the last thing Bo heard
before he fell asleep.

Grandpa woke Bo up and
asked if he wanted to go to
the barn with him.

Bo yelled, "Yes Grandpa!"

"Yes Grandpa!"

"Yes Grandpa!"

Bo got his overalls on and he and Grandpa set off in the truck to the barn.

While in the truck, Bo wanted to know if there were any outlaws, bandits, or pioneers in the West.

Grandpa said, "Bo they were everywhere. The next person I will tell you about is James Beckwourth. He was a pioneer, mountain man, fur trader, and scout. Beckwourth discovered the Beckwourth Pass through the Sierra Nevada Mountains between present-day Reno, California during the California Gold Rush years."

Bo found this fascinating and as he was helping feed grain to the horses,

Grandpa told him about another cowboy.

Grandpa said, "Bo there was another great cowboy by the name of Jesse Stahl. He would put any bronco rider today to shame. Stahl invented the rodeo technique of "hoolihanding" which took a skilled cowboy to do such a task."

Now, Bo was helping throw hay to the horses and thinking to himself how great it would have been to be in the Wild West.

After giving the horses hay, Grandpa LeRoy and Bo were going to fetch the horses water. On the way, Grandpa told Bo about the next cowboy.

Grandpa said, "Bose Ikard, born a slave in Mississippi, thrived on pioneering cattle drives. In 1866, he joined a cattle drive going to Colorado led by Charles Goodnight and Oliver Loving. This became known as the Goodnight—Loving Trail."

Grandpa and Bo got the horses their water and Bo was still amazed.

Bo wondered why he had never heard about these men in history class before.

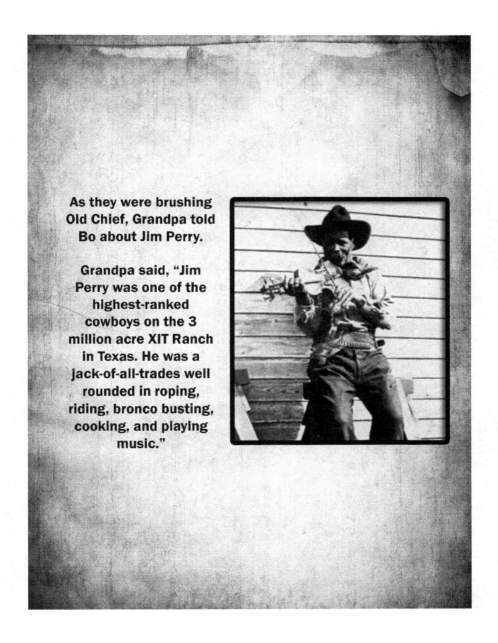

As they were brushing Old Chief, Grandpa told Bo about Jim Perry.

Grandpa said, "Jim Perry was one of the highest-ranked cowboys on the 3 million acre XIT Ranch in Texas. He was a jack-of-all-trades well rounded in roping, riding, bronco busting, cooking, and playing music."

Now it was the end
of their farm chores
for the day and
Grandpa LeRoy had
one more cowboy for
Bo to hear about.

Bo was curious and
couldn't wait.

Grandpa asked Bo if he had ever heard of the song called "Goodbye Old Paint."

Bo said, "Yes Grandpa you sing that song every time we come out to the barn."

Grandpa said, "That was a song by the great cowhand Charley Willis. He was a great cowboy on the Chisolm Trail but he had a deep love for music and that song is one of his most famous."

Bo still couldn't believe it all. The happiness he had was as bright as the sun. Now, the sun was setting and Grandpa made a fire so they could stay out at the barn and gaze into the sky.

Bo said, "Thanks Grandpa LeRoy."

Grandpa LeRoy, "You're welcome Bo. If I don't teach you this history who will?"

Grandpa LeRoy added, "This is just the surface of the 'forgotten cowboys' I will tell you more another day."

Bo looked off into the night sky and gazed at the stars and just started dreaming...

Author Bio

Trae Q.L Venerable, born to Myron and Tracy
Venerable with a life long history in
ranching and farming, is excited to bring
you *Grandpa I Just Wanna be a Cowboy*,
books of the "forgotten cowboys" history.
Trae, an avid outdoorsman, horseman and
cattle jock, comes from generations of
Farm and Ranch owners, from which many
of these stories have been passed on. For
way too long, the "forgotten cowboy" has
not been heard and the time is now.

Visit his website at:
www.traevenerable.com

Coming Soon!

Grandpa I Just Wanna be a Cowboy:
Rodeo Cowboys

CPSIA information can be obtained
at www.ICGtesting.com
Printed in the USA
LVHW022033140221
679287LV00011B/1765